Books by S.C. Giedzinski

Nine Million Marshmallows and More
Island Rain

S.C. GIEDZINSKI

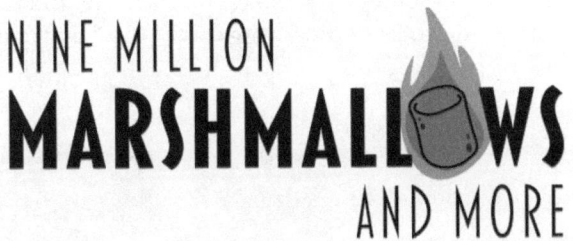

NINE MILLION
MARSHMALLOWS
AND MORE

This book is a work of fiction.

To be more precise, the stories that follow are fictional. This page is not. Names, characters, places, and events in these stories are the product of the author's imagination. Any resemblance to actual events, malicious government agencies, locations, familial curses, other literary works, time-travel phenomena, relatives or friends of the author (living or dead), or anything else in the real world, is purely coincidental. Drink responsibly. Results may vary.

 Brantwood Press

Copyright ©2020 by S.C. Giedzinski

ISBN: 978-1-7348992-0-7

Cover Image © S.C. Giedzinski

For more information, try the damn Internet.

ACKNOWLEDGEMENTS

Eyal Ben-Menachem is an excellent chef. He operates the Gingerbread Fine Restaurant and Boutique Hotel in Nuevo Arenal, Costa Rica. In my life, I have never eaten a better meal than the one he prepared, which was served family-style and included a half-dozen gloriously fresh courses. Chef Eyal had no involvement in the production of this book, but he still deserves to be acknowledged here.

I would also like to thank Johnna Schmidt, Vivianne Salgado, and everyone else in the Jiménez-Porter Writers' House for their help in this project. Additional shout-outs go to Emily Mitchell, Emily Myrick, Howard Norman, Howard Odentz, anyone else named Emily or Howard, Laura Caldwell, and my family, which consists of too many people to be listed on a single page.

As you can imagine, it takes a village to gather nine million marshmallows, so thanks again to everyone who helped out.

CONTENTS

MARSHMALLOWS

Years ago, an urgent message summoned me across several counties to the hospital bed of Dr. Hapthatten, a prominent cognitive scientist. He was a genius by all accounts, and his reputation worried me. Men of science have long feuded with men of the Lord, but even Darwin turned to God at the time of his death. How could I refuse any man's final confession, *especially* that of a scientist? I rushed myself to the hospital where I found him: The odd pantaloon who—as I promptly found out—would eagerly sweep anyone into a lecture of scientific discovery. I never imagined that my lecture from Hapthatten would lead me to fill my church with nine million marshmallows.

The old man shifted his head on the pillow. His voice cracked. "Father, bless me, for I have sinned."

"How long since your last confession?" I asked, as always.

"Years. Too many years." Dr. Hapthatten coughed a few times, and I knelt by the side of his bed to help. He waved me back. "I'm fine, really. Thank you. Well... in these years of my retirement, until several days ago, I'd forgotten a horrible mistake. It happened during a scientific study over fifty-two years ago."

"What was the nature of the study, Doctor?" I feared some horrible malpractice or moral misdeed (I could never tell a soul, of course, if he confessed such a thing). I also feared that he might steer his lecture in the direction of evolution. Thankfully for me, he did not.

"It was a classic exploration of the *Delay of Gratification Paradigm*. In short, we brought in a few hundred toddlers, then we asked them each if they wanted one marshmallow now or more marshmallows later. Simple enough, you see? An adult would have the willpower and logic to wait for more marshmallows. But toddlers will almost always take the first marshmallow right away. Those few who do wait, in theory, will grow to become more determined, patient adults."

"By the grace of the Lord, yes. And you tested the patience of these children, Doctor?"

"I did, with no help from any *Lord*. I offered each child one marshmallow immediately, or one *more* marshmallow for every three minutes that he or she waited. Do you see my mistake yet, Father?"

I shook my head. It disturbed me to kneel by Hapthatten's deathbed discussing something so trivial, indulgent, and sticky as marshmallows. His denial of the Lord disturbed me further. I only wanted to forgive the doctor's sins, not to hear about some old experiment.

Lord, grant me patience, I prayed. He carried on.

"Some of the children who waited earned two, maybe three, extra marshmallows. That data matched my hypothesis, but there was a problem: One toddler kept waiting. Only one. Every three minutes, I placed another marshmallow on his plate, hour after hour, and he never took one! It was *maddening,* not to mention improbable. How could any child be so patient? What marvels would he produce as a tremendously patient and practical adult? I couldn't imagine."

In fact, the scientist could. I didn't sense his cruel scheme.

"What did you do? Did the boy ever take the marshmallows?"

"No. He never did. I sent him home with his parents—sans marshmallows—and I isolated his data from the published set."

At last, I thought I understood. The doctor withheld candy from a child! Yes: A transgression worthy of confession, but the Lord would forgive.

"So Doctor, how many marshmallows did this child earn in your study?"

"His plate held just shy of a hundred when I sent him away."

Perfect, I reasoned incorrectly.

"Shall I try to find him, then? To help make amends? I can repay this boy the proper number of marshmallows! Except… He'll be a middle-aged man now. He'll probably not even remember your study, Doctor. What shall I tell him?"

"Respectfully, Father, you've missed the big problem here."

"What problem?"

"One more marshmallow, *every three minutes*."

I blinked twice. Hapthatten stared at me and waited. I leaned back in my chair, suddenly feeling ill at the thought of so many nasty, rotten, slimy marshmallows.

"No, Doctor. Surely, you don't mean…"

"I've done the math, Father. Fifty-two years' worth of marshmallows. Nine million, one hundred thirty-nine thousand, five hundred sixty-two of them, as of 8:22 last night. Twenty more for every hour that I wait."

I shook my head, refusing to believe the depth of his madness. Could I revoke the proposal I made, only a minute before? Could I so quickly betray my own plan to repay the mounting debt of sugar? No, it was too late, but that number…

"Nine million marshmallows, Doctor?"

Hapthatten's eyes affirmed that this—it seemed—was the one grand confession weighing on his muddled conscience. Thanks to his successful career, Dr. Hapthatten agreed that he could front the money for the marshmallows. He endorsed a blank check, payable to the New Little Haven Catholic Church (memo: *Marshmallows*).

"Fill your church!" Hapthatten ordered. "Gather the marshmallows, then I will reveal the name of the man who's earned them. When the debt is paid, I shall die in peace!"

I left the hospital in a daze and consulted immediately with my fellow priests. While some initially balked at the doctor's request, they eventually perceived some moral soundness in the marshmallow mission. The blank check, they agreed, could also help our small church if needed. With the guidance of the other priests, I began my work of ordering marshmallows in bulk. I hoped to finish the job before the doctor's imminent passing.

The first difficulty involved counting the marshmallows in advance. All websites measured bags of marshmallows in ounces, not in quantity. Would I have to order all the bags and ask my fellow priests to count out nine million gelatinous units?

Lord, grant me patience, I prayed.

By sheer luck, a statistician came for confession the following day. I'd seen him many times at Sunday Mass, and we'd spoken occasionally. In confession, I found a moment to ask him about the growing problem of counting marshmallows, although I tried to phrase my question in a way that sounded hypothetical, or even metaphorical. He hummed in thought like a computer solving some lengthy formula.

"Ah, that's a good question, Father. Each bag will be different. Some will have too many marshmallows, and some too few. It would be impossible to predict the quantity of any bag simply from its reported ounces. But all bags are made to be the same! At any manufacturer, there will be a target average number of marshmallows per bag. A good marshmallow manufacturer will be able to tell you the percent chance of a bag having one, two, or three too many or too few marshmallows, above or below that average. But you'd only know those chances from speaking to the manufacturer."

"Thank you, my friend," I said, rubbing my temples at the growing complexity of Hapthatten's mission.

"It's like people, then, would you say?" The statistician caught me by surprise.

"Hm?"

"The bags of marshmallows are like people. I see! All are made in the same image intended by their Creator. All are truly *created* equal. Our differences are superficial, irrelevant to the greater whole, and only explainable by the Creator Himself. Look at enough people, look at enough bags of marshmallows, and really…"

"They're all the same." I finished for him, trying not to chuckle. He was exactly right, but I had no time for religious insights.

Minutes later, I searched up a direct-delivery website for bulk food products. The manufacturer of the marshmallows (16.5-pound boxes, each containing 24 ten-ounce bags) told me that the bag average should be $33\frac{1}{3}$ marshmallows. This multiplied to 800 marshmallows per box. It was solved! All that remained was to order and pay for the boxes before Hapthatten's final breath.

"You're ordering *how many*?" Asked the woman on the line at the food service.

"I know, ma'am, I don't like the number either: Eleven thousand, four hundred twenty-four boxes."

"To where?"

"New Little Haven Catholic Church."

"Is this a prank call?"

"No, ma'am. I am the pastor of the church. And actually, I'd like to round that number up to eleven thousand five hundred, to be safe."

"Well, Father, if you don't mind me saying, you must really like marshmallows."

"I wish I could say so. Fortunately, they're not for me."

As the woman slowly explained, my next big problem involved the boxes. Each box was 12 inches wide, 18 inches long, and 15 inches high. By her numbers, one of their trucks could hold no more than 385 boxes, if fully loaded. Dividing out eleven and a half thousand boxes necessitated a fleet of at least thirty trucks.

"Thirty?" I stammered, wondering again why I'd accepted the scientist's ridiculous plan.

"Do you have the storage space for this, Father? What about parking? Loading docks?" The woman on the line felt my stress equally, I think.

"I can make it work, somehow. I'll rally our parishioners to help with unloading boxes. And thanks to a very generous donation, we can certainly pay for all of this trouble."

"Very well. We'll have to divert a whole lot of our trucks to reach you, and this will all but *exhaust* our supply of marshmallows, but we can do it on our end."

Wasting no time, I placed the order and cashed Hapthatten's check—in the proper amount, to the chagrin of my mischievous colleagues.

Two days later, New Little Haven awoke to the sound of roaring engines at dawn. A lumbering serpent of thirty food delivery trucks packed tightly with marshmallows emerged over the hills in the west. Never again will anyone in our town witness such an odd spectacle. Only when I saw those trucks did I finally realize that nearby, some unsuspecting man in his mid-fifties would soon receive far more than a lifetime's supply of marshmallows.

Lord, grant me patience, I prayed.

Parishioners turned out in droves, having heard the story of Hapthatten's approaching shipment. The line of trucks parked on the street in front of our church, each driving one by one to the rear entrance, where the able-bodied men and women of New Little Haven unloaded the many boxes. We planned to fill the church basement, and we did that far too quickly. The boxes reached the ceiling, blocking closet doors and leaving only a narrow path through the social hall. Next, we filled the lobby, then the two Sunday school classrooms, before at last we had no choice but to line the pews with marshmallow boxes, all the way up to the altar.

When all was unloaded, our porcelain Jesus gazed down from his crucifix, quizzically surveying his nine million confectionary disciples. Dr. Hapthatten's funds covered the nauseating bill of over six hundred thousand dollars.

But what to do with all the marshmallows?

As soon as the trucks retreated and unblocked our street, I drove back to the hospital to tell Hapthatten the good news. At last, I could send the marshmallows onward to their beneficiary and be done with the scientist's nonsense.

Tragically, on my arrival, I learned that Hapthatten drew his final breath an hour earlier, just as we unpacked the last of the shipments.

"He left this for you," said a nurse, handing me an envelope from the table beside the scientist's empty hospital bed.

I grasped the envelope and tore through the seal, slipping out and unfolding the two papers inside. The first was an informed consent form, signed fifty-two years prior by the parents of a young boy. They'd been paid a swell amount for their son's participation in the study. At the bottom of the page, on the far left, the child's name stood printed on a dashed black line. I propped my glasses up on my nose, reading it over and over.

No, I thought. *Please, God, no!*

On the other paper, a note from Hapthatten:

"I knew you'd do it, Father. Patterns of patience, personality... It's all just science. And years ago, your hatred of marshmallows tested my patience. At last, that favor is repaid. Now go back to your church full of marshmallows, and feast upon your just desserts!"

Never again will I have the *patience* to hear the confession of a scientist.

KINDERSZENEN

"Welcome to Costco," said the uniformed woman, to whom Anna nodded. She didn't say anything back though. Did anyone ever do that? Somewhere distant, a piano chimed gleefully.

"No, mom. Cheetos, not Fritos." A young boy whined, tugging at his mother's leg as she tended to her other child in the cart. Anna wanted to help somehow, but she never had any children. She also didn't know what made Cheetos different than Fritos. Anna wondered if that slight ignorance betrayed her age. It did, she decided, but no more than did the wrinkles at the corners of her eyes. Anna moved along. A shopping cart with a broken wheel rattled past.

Anna reached into her pocket to find no grocery list. No list? No list. Just the cart. God, things were different now. Things would *always* be different now. One of them *always* pushed the cart while the other held the list, so nothing was forgotten. This had been the order of things in Anna's life, but not anymore. The order changes when you lose a spouse, especially after so many decades. Four? That many? Yes, so many, yet not enough. Would all those years together soon be forgotten too? The piano, far off, chirped out another high chord.

Now without the mourning friends, the stoic priest, and the countless relatives, Anna sensed her growing loneliness that began on the night when she left the hospital. With her cloud of grieving comfort now lost, Anna craved not only a return to lucidity, but also a well-stocked kitchen—hence the trip to Costco.

Anna wished for this to be a normal shopping trip, but it couldn't be. If nothing else, the day of the week set this excursion apart. The routine Costco trip *always* came on Sundays after church, and the two of them *always* shopped together. Yes, that was a whole lot of *always*. Anna liked *always*.

There! That piano music again. What song? Anna couldn't remember.

Today wasn't Sunday. Monday, maybe? No, Tuesday, more likely. Another thing, forgotten. Anna didn't know what a Tuesday grocery run should look like. Without a list and without grocery items to count, she instead counted what could be salvaged from her aging cache of half-forgotten memories. There were so many moments she'd lost, and not just in old age. Where did those green-and-red plaid slippers go? What happened to the U-shaped headrest that used to slide around in the backseat of her Volkswagen? How did she manage to lose her blue purse at a production of *The Music Man* in 1987? And why did she lose the DuGrave Foundation Piano Competition in junior high school?

That last memory reappeared in her mind, whole and clear for the first time in years. Anna then remembered *exactly* why she lost that competition. What happened that night? Something important. Something monumental. As Anna began to recall her experience, a sound from that distant piano fluttered into her ears again, clear as day. Did she imagine it? Had she finally metamorphosed into a delusional old widow? Hopefully not. That sound must have come from a real piano, here in Costco. *It is a big store*, Anna told herself, *and Costco sells everything these days*.

Anna ditched her cart and drifted up and down the countless aisles. Stacks of numbered cardboard boxes towered above like her own cluttered memories. Some of the other Tuesday shoppers passed her by, taking no apparent notice. She chuckled, feeling like a ghost wandering the carefully stocked shelves. Would her ghost haunt Costco someday? Had another ghost—a familiar one—already holed up somewhere deep in Costco's labyrinth of aisles?

Every few minutes, the piano called out to her again. She played a sort of hide-and-seek game with the sound. Whenever she felt herself getting closer, Anna sensed something else excitedly creeping towards her from behind. Nothing bad, of course, but something half-forgotten, wild and intangible, like a flash flood or a heartful laugh or the urge to dance.

At last, she turned a corner, and the full memory of that fateful piano competition unrolled like a fog in Anna's mind. The obsidian curves of an expensive display piano rose up in front of her. Who'd been playing it? Where did they go? Did she imagine the sound after all? No, because she'd found the piano, and regardless of how, she knew what to do next.

Don't make a scene, Anna told herself. She unconsciously took her seat on the piano bench, ready to do just that. Anna closed her eyes and let her unthinking fingers sink to the waiting keys. Like a mountain spring, she unleashed her river of memory.

The song: *Opus 15*, Robert Schumann. That iconic, thirteen-part piece outshined her Bach on the last night of the piano competition, so many years ago. Young Anna, seated in the front row of the audience, knew immediately when she lost it all. Her classmate, Carla Maurens, smartly picked *Op. 15*, something imaginative beyond her years and yet fittingly youthful. Young Anna grasped helplessly at the velvet of her auditorium seat, listening with jealousy as delicate notes flowed forth from the open grand piano, which on that stage—on that night—belonged to Carla alone. All felt lost.

Lost, yes, but no longer forgotten.

Each lift and fall of Schumann's piece overflowed from Anna's memory, through her core, to her outstretched arms, and to her fingertips where they danced up and down Costco's display piano. She'd forgotten the grocery list, her slippers, and many other things, but to her surprise, *Op. 15* remained, and she continued to play. With eyes shut, Anna couldn't see the mother and her two children returning to watch and listen from a short distance away.

In Anna's mind, Carla played on, and memory faded into fantasy. Anna's younger self lifted from the seat beside her mother, floating and soaring as if watching the performance from above. From one movement to the next, Young Anna's jealousy and indignation floated away too, replaced by a mature appreciation for her opponent's talent. The piano competition, the months and years of practice after school, and even the gleaming trophy on its table all stepped aside to make way for Carla Maurens and *Opus 15*. Young Anna breathed in every sound and every detail as Carla swayed from side to side, carrying the entranced audience through every second of Schumann's masterpiece.

Now, nearby shoppers did the same for Anna. Her aged hands recalled every note, and she rendered her memory piece by piece through the Costco piano without a single mistake. When the fifth movement echoed out over the store, the greeter from the entrance abandoned her post to come watch the magic.

"Who is she?" whispered the greeter to the mom with the two kids and the Cheetos.

"No idea," answered the mom. "She's unbelievable, isn't she?"

That was rhetorical, so they fell silent. All sound that remained came from Anna's piano. Or, was it Anna's piano?

Behind her two closed eyelids, still reimagining a fantasy of that night decades ago, Anna let her younger self glide across the stage, and the audience vanished. The trophy crumbled away. Only the two of them, Carla and Anna, remained in that empty concert hall. Without missing a beat of the song, Carla opened one eye and cracked a grin at Anna. She tried not to act smug, but Carla glowed with the energy of having already won the competition. Without hesitation, however, she slid over, inviting Anna to join her on the stage's small piano bench. Anna did so. She held her eyes on the keys while Carla concluded the eighth movement. Then, to Young Anna's dismay, Carla grabbed her hand and lifted it up to the keys. Together, they began the ninth movement.

"Do you know the song?" asked the mom to the greeter, who shook her head.

"I hardly even took lessons as a kid."

"She's been playing for a while now. How do you think she remembers all of that music?"

"Muscle memory?"

"I'm looking up the song now," added another employee, having abandoned his post at the free sample cart. "I have an app on my phone that'll say what song it is."

"It's beautiful."

"I feel like I'm at a concert."

"Then we're underdressed."

Anna's whirring fingers danced through the ninth, tenth, and eleventh movements. The sound cast a spell over the few people gathered at the back of that aisle. After all, no one enters a grocery store on a Tuesday expecting to witness such a marvel. Not even Anna anticipated this spontaneous moment when the greeter first welcomed her into Costco. Still playing, Anna marveled at the clarity of her old memory. Like on that night so long ago, Carla again caught Anna—and this time, Costco—by surprise.

"I found the song."

Several heads leaned over the one employee's phone to see. They read the song's name over and over for a few seconds before any of them spoke, and they kept their voices hushed when the twelfth movement of the song quieted down.

"*Kinderszenen, Op. 15.*"

"*Robert Schumann.* He sounds familiar."

"So… German?"

"I would think so."

"*Kinderszenen*, it's called. What does that mean?"

"*Kinder* is child. Like *kinder*garten."

"*Szenen?*"

"I have a translator app. I'll check."

"Listen, I think she's almost finished."

The thirteenth and final movement of *Opus 15* rolled through the Costco aisles. Deep in Anna's mixed memory and imagination, two young rivals threw aside their fierce egos to make music not as enemies, but as allies. Carla struck the chords; Anna filled out the melody. Anna held the shopping list; Carla pushed the cart. Carla gave Anna a pair of green-and-red plaid slippers, and Anna gave Carla a wedding ring. They laughed, they loved, and they grew old together on a piano bench.

"*Kinderszenen*," the free sample man read aloud, "Scenes from Childhood."

Inevitably, *Opus 15* came to a close. Anna faded back into reality to hear a soft round of applause from her little crowd of surrounding listeners. She smiled, blushed, and rose slowly to turn around and bow, but Anna saw no one in front of her. She saw only herself, Carla, and the piano on their stage. Beyond many years, beyond death, these memories lived on through their song. *Kinderszenen* lost, but never forgotten.

BARRY GOES HOME

Barry checked his watch: *12:32*, and his father stepped outside for the first time in thirty years. Barry stood a dozen paces back from the prison door, eyeing the withered man who raised him. Those squinted sunken eyes and that speckled shaved head were all new, but that sour smile was all the same. This was the same man who once climbed a roof to hammer tiles during a thunderstorm, the same man who caught a fruit bat in Barry's childhood bedroom, and the same man who sat long hours on the porch with his rifle, like some minuteman from another age.

Barry stepped forward to embrace this shrunken stranger.

"I'm going home, Junior. Home."

Barry jumped at the sound of *Junior*. He shared his father's surname. Everyone always said *Junior* back in the day.

"It's good to have you back, Dad."

"Geez, your voice," Barry senior said. "I read all your letters, but you haven't called in ages."

"Well, they had you locked up pretty tight in there."

"I had a phone I coulda used. And you know, I heard things have changed a lot out here. Some of the guards told me things. About their families. About whatever crazy new technology is making waves. But I think some of them were just fuckin' with me. C'mon, a colony on Mars? I haven't been away that long!" Barry senior laughed and pointed at the small gray compact parked nearby. "That your car?"

"Just a rental."

"Good. It's ugly as hell."

Barry checked his watch: *12:39*, and the traffic light stayed red for another minute. Not a single car passed from either direction on the wide boulevard ahead. Barry senior craned his head like a groundhog poking up from a hole. Everything he saw, he saw for the first time in three decades.

"Geez, where is everyone?"

"It's easier to go places now. People went places. Even Mars, like you said."

"I'll believe it when I see it. And all that over there, that's new."

"The wastewater treatment plant?"

"Nah, that's always been next to the prison. The state keeps all its shit in the same place, you know? I'm talking about those panels on the field next to it."

"The solar farm? I didn't think it was new."

"Well it is."

The traffic light finally changed, and the car hummed forward. Barry pretended to drive, just for his dad's sake, but his rental car could drive itself as well as any other model. Barry suspected that might frighten his dad.

"Is it Sunday, Junior?"

"No, I think it's Wednesday. Why?"

"There's no one out here. Not even—well, okay, there's one other car. But look, no one on the sidewalks! This road used to always be crowded."

On one side, an old health clinic sat in ruins, its windows smashed. Next to it, an abandoned car dealership showcased a parking lot of cars with all their doors and wheels stolen. On the other side of a road, a *muebleria* boasted "Nobody beats our prices!" on its door, but a discarded mattress covered all but the word "Nobody."

Barry shrugged. "Like I said, it's easier for people to go places now."

"What places?"

"Anywhere they want to go. The most remote and beautiful places. Exotic destinations."

Barry senior rolled his eyes. "Only place I want to go is home."

Barry nodded. "Well alright. Let's just get some lunch first."

Barry checked his watch: *12:53*, and the desolate boulevard branched into a shortcut towards the next town. It was the fastest route to food, and the Dolly-Olly Diner was the last good restaurant in the county. But the shortcut wove through a few miles of overgrown farmland, and Barry's hands gripped tighter on the redundant steering wheel. Barry senior perked up.

"I thought we were going to lunch first?"

"We are."

"But we're almost home. Will they be waiting out on the porch?"

"Well, Dad, no." Barry held his breath.

"I gotta fix my collar. Damn, thirty years!"

"Dad, you've gotta understand. We're not home yet."

"But we're about to be. Geez, slow down! It's right up on the left. You're gonna miss—"

The pointed end of an old farmhouse roof rose between shifting waves of grass. The road led up the hill, and more familiar bits of the hollow building presented themselves. Plywood sheets covered every broken window like skin grown over wounds. One side of the porch roof drooped and knelt to the ground, spilling its gray tiles onto the dusty earth. A vine of some foreign ivy danced up the other side of the awning and trickled into Barry's old bedroom window on the second floor.

"Holy shit," Barry senior spat and drove his fingers along the back of his prison-shaved scalp. "You all moved out? When?"

Barry softened his voice. "Right after you left. The house, I mean, we couldn't keep it. Hell, we never could. Especially after what happened. And all the legal fees, it was too much."

"I built that place, Junior. That's our home."

"It was," Barry nodded. "It sure was."

Barry checked his watch: *1:18*, and still no sand-wiches. In the old days, it didn't take long to make a reuben and a cheeseburger, but times were different. The diner could hardly even stay afloat anymore. Only one waitress remained on the staff at the Dolly-Olly. Barry and Barry senior were the only patrons—but then again, it was the end of the lunch hour.

"Where are you all living then?" Barry senior finally asked. "And don't say Mars."

"Well, I'm with Connie and our kids. We have a big apartment; it's nicer than you expect. Bella's in fifth grade this year, and Tony is in second. I don't know if you've talked to Ellie, but she's out on her own in the Adirondacks. She visits about once a month. And John, has he written to you? He summited Everest last spring with his boyfriend, and now he's in Italy I think, but I don't—"

"Okay, okay," Barry senior raised his hands in sur-render. "I can't wait to meet my grandkids. And Con-nie sounds lovely, from all you've said. All I'm asking is *where*. If you're not at the house anymore, where do you, Connie, and the kids live?"

Barry faltered, and his dad's eyes widened.

"Geez, Junior. Spit it out."

"Hale City."

"Where the hell is Hale City?"

"The middle of Hale Crater."

Barry senior shook his head to re-emphasize his question.

"Mars, Dad. We moved to Mars."

Barry senior snorted. "You're fuckin' with me. Everyone's fuckin' with me. What, like I'm so old I don't know what's real? Like I'll believe anything? Some jackass last year told me kids don't learn to drive cars anymore. Another guy comes in ranting about his watch that lets him fuckin' *teleport*. Real funny jokes, but you try laughing after thirty years locked up. I'm ready to go back to the real world, not some Star Trek fantasy. Why don't you—"

"Dad, hey! Please, just listen. I'm not trying to trick you. Really, this isn't some joke. See that, outside? My ugly rental car? It's gone. Drove itself to a charging station while we eat lunch. And look around! I mean, you keep asking where everyone went, and I keep telling you. See this watch on my wrist? It's for a subscription service that Connie and I pay for. Up to five teleports per month, per watch. We can go *anywhere*, Dad. Adirondacks, Everest, Italy, Mars, anywhere."

Barry senior leaned back on the green faux leather of the diner bench. He breathed deeply once, then twice. Barry tapped his foot on the linoleum floor. Just when his father opened his mouth to talk again, the lone waitress returned with their sandwiches.

"Ah, about time." Barry senior picked up his cheeseburger. He held it in the air and scrutinized it, like an archaeologist studying a fossil. "Do they still have these on Mars?"

Barry checked his watch: *2:25*, which meant that Connie and the kids expected Grandpa Barry at any minute. Barry gave his dad a watch to use, but they ended up standing in the Dolly-Olly parking lot while Barry senior fiddled with the device's settings. However, after an hour standing around, Barry senior still wasn't ready. He voiced some concerns, too. *How do I know this thing won't just take my arm to Mars? Do I have to hold my breath while we're in space? What time is it on Mars, because I have pills I need to take before bed...*

Barry tried to be patient, but he knew his father too well.

"It's okay if you don't want to go," Barry speculated, and his dad recoiled.

"Of course I wanna fuckin' go! I wanna go meet my grandkids, and your wife, geez! I just gotta be sure I know how to use this damn thing you put on my arm."

"It's okay, Dad. If you want to stay here, I can't make you go home."

Barry senior's shoulders sank. The wrinkles under his eyes softened. This was the same man who once fought for their home. This was the man who stood his ground for years and tore up every 'Overdue' notice that landed in the mailbox. This was the man who sat on the porch every day, waiting with his rifle for someone from the bank to arrive. This was the man who rose in defiant shouts when that day came—the man whose gun slipped from his hands, fell to the ground, and fired once through the chest of a bank messenger. This was the man who stood now in front of Barry, changed in a million ways and none at all.

"Dad, I don't know. Maybe, *maybe* there's something we could've done to keep the old house, but it's too late now. The house is gone. The world is different. I know you made that place for us, and I really do wish we could've stayed."

"I fought for that house, Junior. Killed for it, on accident."

"I remember," Barry nodded slowly.

"So let's go back."

"Dad, you saw it. For fuck's sake, it's time to get up off your porch and move on! There's nothing left!"

"Sure there is. We can fix it up. Fight for our home, like we always did. We can—"

Barry pressed his watch's crown and disappeared from the Dolly-Olly parking lot.

Barry senior checked his watch: *3:32*, and it had taken him awhile to walk home. He circled the property twice, planting his shaky feet between uneven patches of grass. The farmhouse was only a hazy reflection of its old form.

The collapsed porch roof couldn't be lifted without a small crane or a front-end loader. He'd need a new job just to rent one, and no one would lend a job—never mind heavy construction machinery—to a felon. The whole roof needed new tiles, and it would take him weeks to install them all. His knees couldn't handle so many trips up and down a ladder, and he'd probably smash his arthritic fingers while hammering nails. The windows could be replaced, of course, but the interior would need cleaning for mold and insect damage. He'd have to hire someone for that. And the vines on the side of the house, which could look nice if trimmed properly, would be a nightmare to maintain. The fight was over, for better or for worse.

Barry senior stepped cautiously onto the front porch where the roof still hung over it. He leaned down, clutching his hip, to search for the wooden rocker where he once sat with his rifle. Evidently, the porch roof crushed it. The rifle, meanwhile, remained archived as evidence in the county police lockup.

He couldn't go back. He couldn't live in the old house again. He couldn't sit outside watching the tall grasses sway in the summer evenings. He couldn't see his sons and daughter graduate from school. He couldn't spend time with his wife before the world lost her. However, he could keep saying *Junior* until Barry demanded he stop. He could meet his grandchildren and his daughter-in-law. He could—for the first time in his life—give up the fight.

Barry senior turned away from the house, pressed his watch's crown, and went home.

TREE OF LIFE

The oak stood leafless for a year before becoming a problem. In his daily rushes to and from construction sites, Marvin overlooked the driveway's dying canopy. Danielle spent her days hunched over self-help e-books, equally unaware of the looming tree. At five o'clock on a Wednesday in September, the oak dropped a branch the size of a coffin. Marvin's gray Nissan wobbled into the driveway at the same second, and its front end bought the whole *shmack* of the tumbling wood. While Marvin forced his crippled vehicle into park, Danielle exited her download of Dr. Larry Henz's *Saving Your Marriage: A Step-by-Step Solution* and rushed outside to her husband's aid.

"Shit!" Marvin knelt over the Altima's crumpled hood, straining to pull the branch aside. Danielle gasped.

"Careful, you'll hurt your back again!"

Marvin glared up at the bare-limbed culprit, whose remaining branches waved over them. "When did this ugly thing die?"

"Oh, I love this tree," Danielle scratched her head. "I thought it was doing fine."

"Then where are all its leaves?"

"Gone for winter."

"Already? It's only September."

"Oh, well isn't that about right?"

"No. The tree's dead, Danielle."

"Oh right, my bad."

Dr. Henz recommended that Danielle try to keep Marvin from getting upset. That was step eleven in the book. Dr. Henz also suggested that she never say the word "sorry;" this was step five. She often found herself looking up synonyms for "sorry." There were no rules against those. As her husband plucked wood chips off his ruined car, Danielle wandered inside and set to work on step fifteen: "Cook a simple high-carb dinner that you can share."

While his wife boiled water for pasta, Marvin jumped into action against the offending oak. He poured some fuel into a dusty chainsaw, which he dredged from the depths of the backyard toolshed. A quick phone call to his union friends brought Marvin a forty-foot scissor lift to reach the tree's highest arms. Like a medieval knight rising to battle a dragon, Marvin rose on the scissor lift's humming platform while angrily tugging at the chainsaw's starter cable.

"Oh, I've made some linguine with garlic pesto!" Danielle called up from the driveway, as if this news surprised her equally.

"You've done what?"

"There's some pasta down here for you, if you'd like."

The chainsaw's engine grumbled to life, cutting their conversation short. Danielle returned to the kitchen, where she scooped a plate of linguine for herself and covered the bowl with aluminum foil. She carried her steaming plate into the living room and reopened her book. Dr. Henz's twentieth step told her to avoid eating smelly foods. Danielle immediately began scraping the garlic pesto from her pasta.

Outside, Marvin dug his blade into the lowest of the decaying branches. Sawdust fell like dry flakes of snow on the steel platform and grassy lawn. Marvin grinned as the first branch cracked, splintered, and snapped from the oak's trunk. It tumbled and crunched to the ground, splitting its fringes into loose twigs. Marvin raised the platform and sawed into the next branch. He kept up this rhythm for almost an hour: Cut, rise, repeat.

Likewise, Danielle kept up her reading. There were so many things about marriage that no one ever bothered to tell her, and Dr. Henz—a thrice-divorced Texas radio host with a PhD in marketing—knew *everything* on the subject. Danielle needed some of that wisdom. Something had changed in the past few years of her marriage, ever since Marvin became a union leader. Was that the reason? Danielle's friend used the term 'mid-life crisis.' That same friend recommended Dr. Henz's book.

The sun rolled lower towards the horizon, peeling away layers of humid midday heat. Marvin had expected to vanquish the tree before nightfall, but the sky darkened hours before sunset. A breeze from the southwest dragged along a thin sheet of clouds. The whole sky soon shifted into grayscale, but Marvin found himself too enraptured by chainsaw exhaust to take notice.

Inside, Danielle snored on the couch with her e-book and plate of quarantined pesto.

The scissor lift buzzed, warning Marvin that he'd achieved his maximum height. He wasn't bothered by this; the only remaining branches were so thin that he could reach out and snap them free with one hand. One by one, they spun and drifted in the wind before landing on the pile below. As one branch fell, a drop of sappy fluid drained from the wounded tree. Marvin took a closer look. There was a hint of green at the center of the ringed wooden gash. It wasn't much, but so far up the tree... What did that mean? Marvin wondered whether the oak could regrow from the brink of death. It would take a miracle. Besides, he'd already cut down so many branches. Marvin revved the chainsaw and decided to carry on.

Unbeknownst to him, the shifting breeze pulled that falling branch a bit closer to the scissor lift's metal base. The stick's thicker end smacked the lift's red emergency button, disabling its power.

Simultaneously, a raindrop smacked the crown of Marvin's head. He set down the chainsaw. From the top of his steel tower, Marvin gazed up at the swirling gray sky. He decided the rest of the tree could wait until the morning, or at least until the squall blew over. However, upon pulling the lever to lower the lift, Marvin found his mechanical assistant unresponsive.

"Danielle!" Marvin shouted down to the empty driveway. He patted his pockets twice, then one more time before remembering where he left his phone in his battered car. Marvin tried the lever again, but the platform held firm. He jumped up and down, shaking the steel contraption. The remaining trunk of the half-dead oak danced a waltz from side to side. Its rough bark squealed and groaned against the lift's railing. More and more raindrops pecked at the hairs on Marvin's head.

Dr. Henz's seventh step said to always remain calm. Danielle knew this, but Marvin had neither read nor heard of the doctor's book, so he grew steadily *less* calm. Lightning concerned Marvin the most, at first. He could hear thunder in the distance already. Would the bolt strike him or the oak trunk? Did it matter, when the two stood so close together? Next, he considered the wind. A gust of thirty miles per hour might send the scissor lift toppling down over his already-crushed Altima.

While the rain steadily soaked his shirt, Marvin devised a plan for escape. He swung a leg over the lift's railing and clung to its opposite side. He reached the toe of one construction boot towards the diagonal crossbar underneath the platform, but his other shoe slipped on the wet metal. Marvin gripped tight onto the railing. His feet dangled in the wind. The growing wind pushed the tree and the lift from side to side, making it difficult for Marvin to pull himself up. His arms felt weak from holding the chainsaw for so long. The rainwater seeped under his curled fingers and begged them to slip free from the railing.

Marvin eyed the tree that got him into this mess. The rainfall began to crescendo. The wind howled and strengthened. The scissor lift hovered on the edge of its tipping point. Dangling over certain death, Marvin ran out of options.

A fantastic *boom* shook the house, and Danielle jolted awake. Her plate of garlic pesto fell onto the carpet.

"Oh!" She cursed and rushed for paper towels to clean it up. Seeing the rain outside—and assuming the loud noise to be thunder—Danielle further assumed that Marvin had already come inside. With a sigh, Danielle dropped her paper towels and wandered upstairs to the bedroom.

The bed was empty.

Sensing something awry, Danielle ran shakily into the tempest outside. She recalled the thundering *boom* that awoke her. Raindrops mixed with her nervous tears, and she could hardly see. She didn't want to see, but there it was: The toppled, crumpled remains of the scissor lift lay in ruin across the driveway. Danielle scrambled towards the sideways platform of the fallen machine but found no sign of her husband.

"Marvin!" She yelled. "*Marvin!*"

"I'm alive!" A voice bellowed. "Up here, I'm al-right!"

Startled, Danielle peered up though the rain at the dead oak trunk, which apparently spoke to her. It seemed that the tree was not so dead after all. Danielle pondered a reply, wiped her eyes, and looked up again into the rain.

"Oh, God!"

"I'm alive!" Marvin shouted again. Forty feet above the driveway, he clung to the bare tree trunk with his arms and legs. Marvin's fingernails dug into the wet bark, and his neck craned aside to peer down at his shivering wife. "Don't cry, I'm alive!"

"Oh, I thought the tree was talking to me!" A burst of thunder drowned her out.

"Get me down!" Marvin begged. "Just call some-one, please!"

In a matter of minutes, the fire department's lad-der truck and an ambulance bounced up the curb and into the driveway. Before long, the firemen carried Marvin down from his perch, and a paramedic wrapped him in a blanket of reflective foil. Two idle firemen investigated the fallen scissor lift. Marvin sat on the rear bumper of the firetruck, shivering. Dan-ielle raced to her husband's side as soon as the para-medics cleared him.

"Marvin! Oh, God, I'm so sorry!" She remem-bered step eleven. "No, I'm *not* sorry! I feel terrible, that's all. There's sawdust all over your nice shirt! I'll put that right in the wash. I need to calm down, I'm annoying. Am I annoying? You can be honest! I won't cry if you say yes. Well, I'm already crying, but I won't cry more! Are you upset? Don't be upset. I just—"

Marvin stood, pulled her close, and kissed her until she stopped shaking.

"Danielle… I'm okay. You're not annoying, and I can wash my shirt later. Did you say something about pasta?"

Danielle nodded. "There's a bowl in the fridge. Are you hungry?"

Marvin kissed his wife again. Her lips tasted like garlic.

"You were right," he confessed. "The tree's still alive. I couldn't believe it, but there was some green in the higher branches."

"Do you still want to cut it down?"

"How about we see if it grows back on its own?"

Danielle took his hand. "Okay. We'll see if it grows back."

FOUR-WAY STOP

Naw, I wasn't scared, per se. Or maybe I was. You'd look at me and laugh, thinkin' what on God's green earth could scare a big old man like me, but I'll tell you what: It was a woman I saw on Scottstown Road. Here's what: You'll hear this story, and you'll feel the same thing I felt. C'mon, here, next round's on me. Four've us drinkin'? Seems about right.

You see, this story is *about* the number four. All about it. Here in the US of A, we've got thirteen; that's our evil number. But not ev'ry country has thirteen as its bad one. China now, the Chinese say it's the number four. The Mandarin word for "four" sounds like the word for "death." So in China, four is death's number. But I say, death knows no borders of man or sea. Four's the number of death, the world round; I learned that on Scottstown Road.

If you've driven that way 'round at night, you know how it is. Scottstown Road makes you feel lost even if you've driven down there a thousand times. Sure, they fixed the asphalt last summer, but this all happened before that. Back when we had that nasty line of potholes by the fire station—and a bunch more, all the way through. You remember those? Damn, I always shifted into the left lane just to save my tires. Almost hit a mailman once!

That night though, I was headed back south from jury duty up in the city. Some bum walked free on a hit-and-run. Not enough evidence, We the Jury said. Helluva thing that was. Not the courthouse, really, but the whole city, I mean. Takes a lot out of you just bein' there a few hours. The noise, the buses, the *buildings*. Nothin' like it 'round here. People 'round here know how to keep to themselves, most of the time. I like that.

So I picked up a cheeseburger and left the city as soon as Uncle Sam relieved me of my *judicial duties*. Rush hour traffic part-way killed me. By the time I made it past the plaza and into Scottstown, the sky was more orange than blue.

I drove 'round the potholes by the fire station, then 'round the bend into the backwoods. Next I came to the four-way stop—the one at Harrier Road. You know that one; we all know it. But if it weren't for those electric signs just before, you'd never see it comin' from 'round that overgrown bend right there. Seriously, they put up two flashin' yellow diamonds three hundred feet back. Waste of our taxes, right? I sure thought so.

Anyway, I saw that intersection ahead, and I decided not to stop. Stoppin' always felt weird anywhere on Scottstown Road, especially with no other cars 'round. And there were no cars that eve-nin', so I said oh, I'll just carry on through. I guess that was a bad habit, maybe. I never cared for a law when that law ain't doin' no one no good.

Then this woman walked right out in front of me. Because of her in my way, I had to stop real quick. She came out of nowhere, and she had on this long black dress. Not a real nice one or nothin', but nice enough that I remembered it. And she was barefoot, that too I remember. She walked across the asphalt real slow, sorta wincin' with ev'ry step. Because of the gravel pebbles, I guess. She didn't look like the type who would go out barefoot.

I let her cross the four-way stop, and I started to press on the gas again; I wanted to get home before dark. She waved me down though, so I stopped again, and I rolled down my window to ask what the hell she'd stopped me for. That's when I saw her face: Pale, too pale. Not pale like too little suntan, but pale like somethin' *wrong*. The sort of pale that no one wants to see. But there I was, stopped with my window down, and what was I gonna do, speed off?

She asked if I saw *him*. Him? I don't know who. She didn't know his name, just asked if I saw *him*. Where *he* went. Someone who she was lookin' for. I thought maybe it was some gospel thing, like her takin' a walk and lookin' for Jesus in the Scottstown woods, right? I told her I hadn't seen anyone for miles, and she should get herself home before dark. Then I asked if she needed a ride. At least I tried to ask, but she wouldn't have it. She said that she needed to find *him*, whoever he was. She needed to talk to *him*.

So I left. Just kept drivin', and that was that. I hardly wondered where she went. I rounded the next curve through the woods, thinkin' about how it looked a lot like the one from right before the four-way stop.

You ever get that weird chill-like feelin' in the back of your head when somethin' is about to happen, yeah? Well, I felt it just then. I felt it real strong, and it got loads worse when I saw two flashin' yellow diamonds just ahead. The *same* two yellow diamonds.

I can't explain it any better. I came right back up to the four-way stop at Harrier Road. I know! Quiet, quiet, lemme say it all first.

It was the same direction drivin', just like I'd driven in a big circle. So I thought maybe I'd dozed off and imagined it all the first time. The woman in the black dress, too. It just didn't make sense otherwise. I never took any turns; I had just driven straight, then without really thinkin' anythin', I was right back at the same damn stop sign. And I swear, I never stomped down on the brakes harder. I was freaked.

Ev'rythin' looked just about the same, save for a truck that was there right then. It was a white tow truck with a blue company name painted on the side. Somethin' with a cursive *K*, like *Kronum* or *Kronos* maybe. That wasn't what *really* caught my eye, though. The truck was haulin' this wrecked sedan. Broken windows, and really badly dented like it'd rolled. Right when I pulled up, the truck lurched forward and hauled the sedan out of the drainage ditch, right there. I swore that the wreck wasn't there when I *first* showed up at Harrier Road. I would've noticed. But maybe the woman in the dress had distracted me? Or was that first time all in my head, like I thought? You see, I really don't know. But it doesn't end there.

As soon as I let the truck pass in front of me, headed west, there she was again. The woman, I mean. Pale as ever, barefoot, and in that black dress. She didn't ask me to roll down my window this time. She didn't *have* to ask. I parked my damn truck right in the intersection and stepped out to ask her what happened.

I asked, was that her car bein' towed, and she nodded without lookin' at me. Then I could tell she was in shock, that's what it was. I knew somethin' had been wrong the first time, but I guess it was that she'd been in a wreck. She must've been waitin' for the tow truck the first time, right? But then how'd I come to the same spot twice? Still gotta explain that.

Save for her missin' shoes, she looked about unharmed. Still pale as a white rabbit, though. She kept whisperin' somethin' to herself. Some stuff about *him* or where *he* went. That gave me chills, tell you the truth, because right then I saw there was no one else 'round. Whoever hit her car must've sped off, I thought. It made me mad, especially after seein' some guy get away with the same crime at jury duty, remember? That's what it was, hit-and-run.

So I told the lady that the cops'd find the bastard, but she shook her head, and who was I to disagree? I should've stuck 'round longer I guess, but I had to get home, and her mutterin' gave me the creeps. I felt a bit sick; I could taste that horrible fast food cheeseburger from an hour before. So I got back in my truck, hopin' that my eve-nin' would somehow improve.

I left the intersection for the *second* time, cruisin' down through the woods towards home, but I got that feelin' again. Spine rattlin' like wind chimes, and my forehead startin' to sweat cold. This time, I knew what was about to happen. When I came to the flashin' yellow diamonds, I knew it wasn't in my head. I was back *again* at Harrier Road, like I was just roundin' the bend for the first time. I cursed out loud to myself, and that's when I saw the red and blue lights.

Lots of them. A bad sign.

When I stopped at the intersection, a cop car sat just off to my right, and an ambulance waited on the other side of the road. I sat up higher and looked across the way into the drainage ditch, and there was the *wrecked sedan*, like the tow truck had just brought it back! I couldn't believe my eyes. I know! What the hell, I'm thinkin'.

I threw my truck into park and jumped out, leavin' the door open. I half expected the cop to stop me, but he was busy talkin' into his radio. He looked at the ambulance, and so did I, and that's when I saw her. There she was: The woman, barefoot in her black dress, sprawled out on the road.

Dead.

I just watched; I couldn't move, and a paramedic dropped a white sheet to cover her.

It's unnatural to see someone dead right after you've seen them alive. But then I started to wonder what I really *had* seen. Because now, the sedan was back in the ditch. The tow truck... What, it hadn't come yet? That's when I started thinkin' maybe I'd been seein' this whole thing in the wrong *order*. Nothin' else ever felt as eerie or as sickenin' as that idea, I swore. But right then, somethin' even worse happened. I heard the woman talk behind me:

"Where did he go?"

And I didn't need to look over my shoulder. There she was again, the woman. Back from the dead to attack me, I knew it. A ghost. A real, *real* ghost. I damn near screamed, and I know I must've jumped halfway out my skin. All the air 'round me turned cold, and I ran back into my truck as fast as I could.

I flew outta that intersection faster than ever, and I never took my foot off the gas. This... this rabbit hole must have a way out, I decided. So I said to myself, I'll gun it 'round ev'ry curve until I'm home safe. Hell, I'll close my eyes if I come 'round to that four-way stop one more time. That night, I was on the run from the woman in the black dress, and no flashin' yellow diamonds were gonna slow me down now.

Him, I thought. Where *did* he go? What happened to this woman? Why did her spirit choose *me*? And why did ev'rythin' seem so mixed up?

The chills kept comin'. Full-body terror, I think that's called. Alarms rang in my head so loud, I thought it was the fire station. I shook and shivered and pressed the gas pedal to the floor. As I got closer to that four-way stop, I saw no tow trucks. No ghosts, no cops. No woman in no black dress. I thought I might almost be free, if I just passed through one more time. I thought I'd outrun whatever evil took hold of me. I wasn't thinkin'.

I stopped at Harrier road four times that night.

The first time, I saw her ghost. The accident was cleaned up.

The second time, I *met* her ghost. The tow truck left.

The third time, I *heard* her ghost. And she was dead on the asphalt.

The fourth time was the last time. The *death* time.

Do you see it now, the number of death? Do you see how it played for me like a movie in reverse? Well, I didn't see it. I just acted out my role, and I didn't even know it. Ev'rythin' happened too fast. I came into the intersection, engine roarin', and there was no time to react. I barely saw the sedan's headlights. Tires screeched. A near miss! Behind me, metal scrapin' asphalt, glass shatterin'. A scream, then nothin' at all.

By the time I stopped and ran back to the intersection, it was all gone. No sedan, no woman. Like nothin' happened. I looked for some clue that it'd all been real, that it hadn't just been in my head. I found nothin'. I can't prove what I saw, and I don't think I ever will. As far as anyone can say or tell, that night there were no accidents at the four-way stop.

But there is one thing I figured out. Remember how the woman asked where *he* went? The man who ran her off the road? The man who killed her. The man who chose not to stop, like he had his eyes closed. Well, I found that man. And he's right here talkin' to you.

Yeah, I know. Another round, four drinks, who's to stop us?

ED

Edward Norbery often reassured himself that the Curse afflicted his family, not just him. Ed knew that lots of families claimed to have curses, but the Norbery Family Curse proved itself without fail from the moment he entered the world—five days late.

Ed began primary school a year late because his father turned in the wrong forms at the district office. Ed grew up as an only child because his parents were already too old to try for another. Ed's father never made it home in time for dinner—traffic, always— but fortunately for him, Ed's mother rarely served dinner on time either. For so many years, the Curse held illimitable dominion over all.

When Ed graduated high school a year late, his diploma arrived another six months later due to a printing error. Having missed most college application deadlines, Ed took a gap year to travel abroad, but he soon gave up travel due to his expensive pattern of missing flights. Again thanks to the Curse, the gap year mistakenly became a *pair* of gap years before Ed finally entered community college, where he failed his first semester due to "Frequent Tardiness."

All the while, Ed tried to remedy this issue. He truly did. Ed's father, after all, was a postman who'd taught him the values of patience and perseverance. Ed set hundreds of alarms, but they rarely rang at the proper hour. Ed asked friends to wake him in time for class, but they never remembered to do so. At last, Ed gave in to the Curse, and he prepared to enter the workforce.

On that day, the twelfth of March, Ed drove himself to a job interview scheduled for ten in the morning. Traffic, for once, abated. Lights turned green and stayed that way. His car's tires neither popped nor deflated. No freak hailstorms emerged overhead. Ed marveled at this relative serendipity, laughing joyfully and wondering if this might be how everyone else always felt. Proudly double-checking his watch, Ed parked his car and strolled slowly into what he hoped would be his new workplace.

"You're here," spoke a man at the reception desk. "It's about time."

"Yes, it is! Just about time." Ed checked his watch once more. Still five minutes until ten.

"Look," the man replied, pointing to the wall behind Ed.

There, above the door, a digital clock corrected the time to 10:55. Ed buried his face in his hands: *Daylight savings!* The Curse remained unbroken.

And Ed laughed nonetheless.

BLINKERS

In the high mountains of western Montana, tucked between the silent slopes of pines, a two-line railway cut its slithering path from east to west. Every hour, thundering metal wheels carried so many tons of coal, grain, oil, or automobiles through an otherwise empty wilderness. The railway was my river—incessant, violent, and unstoppable. I knew every curve, tree, hillside, and house like the back of my hand.

One hazy Monday morning, I drove a hundred-car coal train through a high pass in those mountains. Smoke from nearby wildfires hung over the sleepy town at the top of the ridge. My engine barreled onward through the peak of its climb, beginning to pick up speed as the tree line thickened once again. I rounded a slow curve as the rails swept downward. Suddenly I spotted an obstruction on the tracks ahead. I reached for the air brake, but my hand wavered. There was no time. Through the clearing wildfire smoke, I stared in awe at the tracks ahead.

A woman sat cross-legged between the rails, raising both hands as if to say *Stop*. I would've reacted right away, but the chilling sight of her prepared-ness—her absolute calmness—held my attention for a few extra moments. My train hammered closer, closer, and closer. She never moved. Never turned around and kept her palms extended towards me.

I shut my eyes.

I was young when I first jumped through time by mistake. I reached for a drinking glass on a high kitchen shelf, knocked it onto the counter, and it shattered. My mother came running downstairs at the sound.

"Oh!" she gasped and pulled me away from the wreckage. Blood oozed from a cut on my right palm. A piece of glass stuck deep in the red gash. I knew that as soon as my mom bandaged the wound, she'd turn on me. *You should be more careful! You'll use only plastic cups from now on!*

I blinked and found myself standing back at the counter. Just like seconds earlier, my arm reached up at the same glass on the high shelf. But the counter was still clean. My mom was still upstairs. I drew my hand back and called for her to come help me reach. Meanwhile, I checked my hand. No cut, no blood. I thought about this for days afterwards, but I never tried to explain my experience to my mom.

After high school, I worked at a model train store. I always liked the precise mechanical systems that allowed tiny locomotives to function. Over time, I saw the even greater beauty in rail travel: Complete and unquestionable control. The rails hold an elaborate physical system in perfect balance. The train moves forward, and its predestined path is assured by its rails to be perfect.

Unlike mine.

One night, as I drove my car home from the model train shop, a storm blew in from the south. The narrow road had no streetlamps, and my headlights hardly penetrated the rain. As I passed through a forest near my house, a large brown dog leapt in front of my car. She struck the hood and crashed through the windshield before her paws even landed on the pavement.

Dogs make the most awful noises when they die.

I blinked myself back thirty seconds and slammed the brakes. I hydroplaned at least a hundred feet before stopping sideways on the empty road. This time, the dog stepped safely out of the shadowy trees. She stood in the road, feet away from my car, and her dark black eyes met mine through the rain. For the first time, my ability saved a life. I discovered—by accident—a more perfect path. I soon became a train conductor.

I opened my eyes.

Two miles further back in the mountain range, clear of the suicidal woman, I casually applied the train's brakes. I glanced up from my controls and beamed through the front window—in horror.

She was back, unmistakably. The same woman sat peacefully in the same position, far back from where I first saw her. Her curled brown hair danced loosely in the mountain wind while my freight train sprinted towards her. I had no room to slow down. I needed a mile, maybe four thousand feet to slow from my speed.

I desperately blinked again, this time rewinding myself all the way back to the first city on my route. My mountain surroundings transformed into towering apartments, parking lots, and car dealerships. She followed me, nonetheless. This time, the woman sat on the tracks at a road crossing, where a dozen stopped cars frantically honked their horns at her. She never flinched. She never turned to face me.

"Damn it!" I shouted and blinked again.

I returned my train all the way to the rail yard, early in the morning before my departure. The engine idled, waiting for me to disengage the brakes. Ahead, the woman appeared again. This time, she stood between the rails facing me with hands planted on her hips. I shut down the engine and stepped out of my cab.

"You look too young to be a conductor," she called up to me. I began climbing down to the gravel.

"You look too young to die," I replied. Her smile gleamed white in the morning sun.

"And who are you to decide that? Why do you choose who lives and dies?"

"Who are you?" I ignored her. "How did you follow me back here?"

She pursed her lips and shook her head. "Have you eaten breakfast yet?"

"I wait til lunch usually. Why do—"

"There's a little cafe place at this rail yard. Want to grab a bite while they fix your train?"

"Fix my... What?"

"I disconnected the brake lines on the last thirty cars. We should have about an hour while the rest of your crew fixes it up."

She started across the other rails towards the employee cafe. I followed slowly. Meanwhile, eight of the other yard workers rushed to the back of my train to reconnect the sabotaged brakes. Their orange reflective vests glowed like sparks of fire.

In the years following my near-accident with the dog, I learned the ropes of my time-blinking skill. There were limits, for sure. I could only jump backward, never forward. Most importantly, I could only ever jump alone. I couldn't take anyone or anything with me. As I tested and practiced and learned my ability, I came to see it less like time travel and more like a rewind button.

Needless to say, I cheated my way through high school. After every test, I discussed answers with my peers before jumping back to the start of the test and avoiding my mistakes. I had good luck in dating, too. Whenever I said the wrong thing, I jumped back a few seconds to try something else. It was as easy as blinking my eyes. For years, I wasted my ability in these ways.

The day after I saved the dog's life, I quit my job and applied to become a train conductor. After all, there was only one flaw in rail transportation, and my unique ability offered a solution.

The problem was momentum. Each freight car weighed a hundred tons. The trains I drove carried a hundred cars or more. It's hard to imagine encountering a twenty-million-pound vehicle that's over a mile long. It's even harder to imagine operating one—or harder still, stopping one. So what would happen if an obstacle fell in the perfect and unstoppable path of a freight train? Nothing good, according to my research.

My train's route took me through two major cities, the mountain range, and dozens of smaller towns. It was ideal, but the obstacles began on day one. On my first day at the controls of a train alone, a black bear's foot became stuck between two rail ties at the foot of the mountains. I pulled the brakes, blared the engine's horn, and flashed the headlights, but the bear couldn't move away. Seconds before impact, I blinked. Minutes earlier, the bear was still a mile ahead. I slowed the train to a crawl. When I reached the same place on the tracks near the mountains, he was gone. I must've bought him enough time to pull himself free.

In my first three months with the freight company, I had the cleanest safety record of any conductor. No reported incidents. It was unheard of: No cars stuck at ground crossings; no animals struck on the tracks. The path of my train was perfect.

"God loves you," said one conductor when he saw my papers. "Consider yourself blessed."

"How long have you been doing what you do?" the woman asked. I found her in the empty employee cafe, which more closely resembled a break room. She shuffled items around in the refrigerator, talking with her head still inside it.

"Working for the railway? I've been here eight years," I said. I took a seat at one of the three tables.

"That's incredible. So every time something goes wrong on that freight line, you blink your eyes, and your million-ton metal monster zaps back to the past? Sounds too good to be true. What's the catch?" She held up a carton of orange juice from inside the fridge. "You want any?"

"There's no catch. It works perfectly."

"Do you want the juice or not?"

"No thank you."

"Vitamin C, potassium. Good stuff," she muttered while pouring a glass for herself. "I want to make sure I understand correctly. Let's say I'm trying to kill myself. I sit down in front of your train, you blink away once you see me, and the train stops miles before it can smash my body into bits. Right?"

"That's the idea."

"And you're sure it works?"

"Yes," I nodded.

Two weeks after my encounter with the bear, a man jumped in front of my train while I passed through the first city on my route. Maybe he just wanted to cross the tracks. Maybe not. Either way, I didn't react fast enough. Other days, I always blinked before impact, but he was too quick. The man disappeared under the engine's front end. The cab jolted, but the train kept rolling. Finally, I blinked.

This time, I stopped short of where the man first crossed. He wandered slowly up the gravel embankment, looked up at me in the idling engine, then crossed solemnly to the other side. I hoped he took it as a sign—either a sign to be more careful, or a sign that his life wasn't meant to end that day.

"How do you know all about... You know, the blinking?" I asked, rubbing my temples. "Who are you, anyway?"

She sat down across the table and sipped from her orange juice. "Ah, gross. There's no pulp in this. But to answer your question, it was a bit of a lucky guess. You see, a few months ago, my husband's supervisor caught him drinking on the job. He didn't tell me that he got fired. He didn't tell anyone. Instead, he shot our two daughters with a hunting rifle and then tried to kill me." The woman grinned, and I shivered. "But he didn't get me. I escaped, I fought back. I saved my daughters and sent my husband to jail. Do you understand how I did this?"

"No, I really don't! You tried to kill yourself, you followed me here, you sabotaged my train, and now you're stealing from the employee fridge. I don't care about whatever craziness happened with your family. What are you doing here?"

She smiled again. "I wasn't trying to kill myself. I just needed to get your attention. I'm like you." The truth hit me like a diesel freight engine. "I can blink like you can. Don't you understand? I blinked when my husband attacked me, and I drove my daughters to safety before he ever shot them. A perfect escape, isn't it? Now, let's take a look at what's happened today. Each time I step in front of your train, you blink us back to safety, and I survive. Each time I survive,

I blink myself back in harm's way, and I sit further up the tracks. We are a paradox."

"Oh," I said. That was all I could really manage. "Why didn't you just tell me that? You know what I do, then. You know how many people I've saved. We can save more lives together! If we both use our abilities to cheat death, we can help the world in ways that I probably haven't even considered."

The woman laughed. Her head rolled back, and she nearly fell over laughing. I must've missed the joke.

"Ha! Well, why don't you tell me, how many lives have you saved? How many people have tried and failed to die by your train?"

"Okay, listen. In my first year as a conductor, three people walked in front of my train. That was above average for any conductor, and I knew that. But I saved all their lives, so I never reported those incidents. In my second year, the number more than doubled, but only for me. Again, I never had to report these. I blinked them all away. The next year, a new person walked in front of my train every other week. No one at the company would've believed the number of people who tried it. It only happened for me, not for any other drivers. By my count, the deaths of so many people would've represented a *significant* percentage of all rail suicides in the country—but they never died. I saved them all. My path was perfect. What are you so upset about?"

With no warning, the woman flipped the table towards me and rose from her chair. The glass of orange juice spilled onto me and shattered across the floor. She lunged forward and grabbed my neck with incredible strength. I grasped at her forearm and kicked my legs in panic, but she forced me across the room with ease. My feet dangled inches off the floor. She held my neck against the wall with only one hand. Her other drew a knife from an unseen holster on her back.

"You don't save lives!" She seethed through gritted teeth. She angled the knife up at my face. "I watched my children *die* because of you! It took me a long time to figure out what drove my husband out of his mind. I had to blink back over and over, dozens of times. Do you know what I discovered? He parked his truck on a railroad crossing, the same day he got fired. The train stopped before it hit him, and that small miracle gave him more time to think. He decided he couldn't leave his family behind. He decided to take us with him... All because *you* decided to save his life! So now, Unstoppable Force, meet Immovable Object."

Her knife dove towards my chest. I didn't feel her stab me, but I felt the *thump* as the blade's hilt struck my chest. The knife cut between my ribs and straight through my heart. The woman's hand tightened on my neck, and I couldn't breathe. A chilling numbness seeped across my body, starting at my fingertips and creeping inward. She twisted the knife. Fiery pain exploded across my chest.

"Close your eyes," she hissed. "One last time, close your eyes, and imagine how many people you've killed to keep your *perfect path*."

I fought to keep my eyes open, but I only had seconds left. This room would be the last place I ever saw. The refrigerator, the tables and chairs, the spilled orange juice, and this woman would be the last thoughts to enter my mind. My eyelids slid down across the twinkling bits of glass on the floor. Darkness.

Unless...

My eyes opened. I stood again at the kitchen counter of my childhood home. Just like before, my young arm reached up at the same glass on the high shelf. The counter was still clean. My mom was still upstairs. I stretched myself up, poked at the tall glass, then let it fall and shatter on the counter. Behind me, a young girl stood watching. Her hair fell across her shoulders in loose brown curls. She smiled warmly and reached behind her back.

I stabbed two glass shards through her eyes before she could blink. The large knife slipped from her limp hand and clattered to the floor. Blood dripped from my palms. I stood, unblinking, over her body.

And over my perfect path, I shut my eyes.

YOU'RE A WINNER

There you are! It's about time. Don't look so surprised; you knew I was on my way. I emailed you. You remember, we emailed. You saw, didn't you? Shit. Oh, that's not good. Well if this building hasn't had Internet in three days, you haven't heard the news. You haven't heard! I should come inside. Yes, excuse you. I'm coming inside.

Oh, wow. Really, this is your apartment? We're gonna have to tidy up a little, aren't we? Do you live alone? That figures. Got family living nearby? Oh. I understand. What a shame. My kids won't speak to me either.

Give me a second to take off my coat. I've got the email right here on my phone. I'll read it out to you. One second. Yeah, here we go: 'Dear Lucky Contestant, On behalf of myself, the United States Entertainment Commission... blah, blah, network partners, corporate sponsors, blah, blah... congratulations! You have been selected as this month's winner of the Instant Celebrity National Lottery. In a few days, we will send a press team to your residence and begin your journey into fame. In the meantime, please be patient, and do not disclose this information before meeting… Blah, blah, whatever.'

You get the picture. You're this month's big winner, and we're gonna make you famous. No, this isn't a joke. I have all your paperwork on file, and everything is in order. Who am I, then? Like you don't know? I'm your fame advisor! Don't worry, I've been in the business for almost ten years, going all the way back to the passage of the Federal Celebrity Management Act and the founding of the U.S. Entertainment Commission. I've got a great team of experts working for me, too. They're on the way up with some basic equipment. They would've come in with me, but apparently your building's elevator is broken.

While we're waiting a minute, did you opt-in to the cancelation insurance policy that USEC recommends? It was a little check box, right on your lottery form next to the terms and conditions. Not necessary, but it is recommended for anyone who's newly famous. You know, if you've got skeletons that might slip out of your closet. No judgement. We've all been young, right? Okay, we can't force you to opt-in. I didn't see any red flags on your background check. Big points to you; you're neither a racist nor a rapist.

And here they are now! Go on and open the door for my team.

(Come on inside. Yeah, I know it's a mess. Stevie, get the servers up and plugged into the generator. You can run it on the back porch. Yeah, it's a small apartment, I know. Nancy and Andrea, get our client into hair and makeup. We have a *lot* of work to do.)

So what's your look? We need to nail down your style before we reveal you to the world. Are you the straight edge working stiff? Or a rough blue-collar underdog? Maybe something younger. You can't be that old, can you? Twenty-five? I don't care, you're twenty-five.

(Davis! Hop on Wikipedia and get our client's page online. Age twenty-five, make sure it says so.)

So you're still young. You can be modern, avant-garde! 80s throwback jackets, flashy colors. Unless you'd prefer something darker, to keep with the times. I mean, the world's probably ending soon, isn't it? Plenty of celebrities tend towards a goth look; it keeps them mysterious or edgy in the public eye. We can put together anything you'd like to try, but first I want to see what you have here already. Take me to your wardrobe. Where is it? Oh, you're kidding. It's only that pile? In that corner, that's *all* of your clothing?

(Benny! Hey! Toss all those clothes in a bag. Donate them, burn them, whatever. Send Maria and Jaden down to the mall, and have them bring back something for our client to wear in public. Make it flashy, but relatable.)

People want to connect with celebrity style, but they don't want to be disgusted. Oh that's no offense to you; I'm sure those rags looked great a few seasons ago.

(Francine, toss me a mirror!)

Here, see what Andrea's done with your hair? Are you kidding? Long hair is out, the shorter looks are in. Don't worry, you'll get used to it. Okay, fine. It'll grow back. We can get you a wig, if you really want.

(Owen! Call up your buddies at *Hair Weekly*, see if they want to sponsor a wig for our client. No, not anything ridiculous. Just make it look like it was before. When? Two minutes ago, before Andrea chopped it off!)

There's someone I need you to meet. This is Robin, she's here with *Vogue*. Tell her about your skincare routine. Oh. Oh no. Okay, do not tell her that.

(Robin! Write up something believable, and we'll buy the products to make it a new daily routine for our client. It's not fake news, come on! It's prenews!)

Moving right along, here's Tom from *Buzzfeed*. He needs your Twitter handle. You'll be verified in a couple hours, and he's gonna put out a list of your sixteen all-time funniest tweets before then. A private account? Jesus, do you even *want* to be famous? Get out your phone and make it public. Better yet, give me your password. There. I'll have Reggie take care of that while you talk to Jamie. Jamie's a correspondent with NBC. He just wants a real quick word from you on the current state of affairs in Gaza. What do you think of a two-state solution? Are you a Zionist? Oh, really. Hm, I never thought of it all like that. It doesn't have to be so complicated! As a celebrity, you have to be political. People love strong opinions. You can take a vague stance as long as you never change it.

(Reggie! Here's our client's Twitter password. Make it public, change the bio, fix the profile and header photos. I don't care, anything that won't make my eyes bleed. We'll take proper headshots in a few minutes. Oh, already? Excellent.)

Great news! We just rolled out your introductory posts on USEC's social media. You have two—no, *three* thousand new Twitter followers, five hundred Facebook friend requests, and eight hundred new followers on Instagram. There are some mentions of you on TikTok, so you're clearly popular with the kids. You also have an unofficial fan page. We'll make an official one, too.

(Ah, Henry! Yeah, we've got a second. Come on over here.)

This is Henry. He wants you to hold this. No, don't drink it, do you even know what's in that can? Alright, say cheese. Perfect. One more. Another. Now a silly one. Love it. We're putting you in an ad campaign for this new energy drink. Yeah, the one you're holding. It uses a new synthetic stimulant that isn't FDA regulated yet. Kids love it, and there have hardly been any deaths, so the ad campaign will be a breeze. And you'll make your cut of the money, don't worry. Ten percent, I think. Fifty for Henry's company, twenty for me, five for USEC, ten for the networks, and five to the compensation fund for the families of the victims. We'll put your name on that too—make you look charitable.

(Henry, you hear that? Ten percent for our client. No funny business like last time.)

What's that on your phone? Oh, you have a text message. Show me who it's from. Really? That jealous hag is your mother? Hey, back off. I'm not assuming anything. It's perfectly obvious. You told me that your family doesn't talk to you anymore, yet here we are: Ten minutes later, there's a text from Ma. Don't let the "Congratulations" fool you. If the old woman has any sense at all, she knows how much advertising money you'll earn by the end of this quarter. You remember Hal, the bicyclist from San Francisco who won the lottery last February? He made eight million bucks from his first two months of Peloton ads. You remember what happened next? His daughter cut the rear brake wire on his seventeen-speed. Next morning, Hal went flying down Bradford street and launched himself through the window of grocery shop. By the time the police figured out what his daughter did, she already blew her whole inheritance on stilettos and cocaine. Is your mom gonna do something like that too? Maybe. So don't talk to her.

There's nothing wrong with being unattached, you know. That's what got you here! Most people in healthy long-term relationships don't play the Instant Celebrity National Lottery. Clearly you want more for your life. You want excitement, and we're here to provide. What? Say that again; I was talking over you. Oh, so you *are* seeing someone! But not really? *Talking*, what does *talking* mean? Show me a picture of this crush you've got. Pull up Instagram. Come on, you're joking. You're chasing someone who looks like *that*, and who only has five hundred followers? Don't be stupid, you can do better. Come on, you're famous now. We'll make you a match that you can't refuse. Remember the lottery winner from last August? No, not the one whose nudes leaked. No, not the one who overdosed. I'm talking about the one with the tall hair and the arm tattoo. Here, see? There's a good picture. Out of your league? You're hilarious. You really do make me laugh.

(Tamara, you hear that? Our client doesn't wanna get with last August's winner. I know, that's what I said! Let's make it happen. Set them up for a date next Tuesday. Pick a good place in Manhattan. Tip off your friends at TMZ, and make sure they get plenty of photos from at least three blocks away. Or just deepfake their faces onto some other couple. You can photoshop the whole thing? Then do that; that's perfect. Cancel the date, just leak the photos to TMZ.)

Okay, alright, quit blabbering about this low-life crush of yours. You can't date someone who isn't a celebrity too. That's the fastest way to stop being famous. People want to see romance, scandals, and debauchery, but only between people they love and understand. Whoever you're *talking* to is now—I'm sorry to say—just another one of your adoring fans.

A speck on your radar, just like your mom. Can you send one last direct message, just to be clear that you're breaking things off? Actually, never mind. I'll have Reggie take care of that for you. Don't be so dramatic; you'll get over it.

(Gertrude, what's our client's schedule for tomorrow morning? What about *Good Morning America*? You're kidding. Since when are three morning shows 'more than enough?' Get ABC on the line, see if they can cut that awful climate activist from tomorrow's lineup. Katy! Get the jet ready, and file a flight plan for New York this evening. Rob, book our client a suite at the Ritz-Carleton for tonight and tomorrow. We are in press tour overdrive for the next forty-eight hours! Cynthia, do you have any spare Adderall on you? Powder some more in my water bottle, will you? And make a separate one for our client. Hey! Gene, where's our client? Attention! Has anyone seen—)

Ah. There you are. Where do you think you're going? No, you can't leave! Fresh air, really? I've heard that excuse a million times. Get back inside! You can't be seen in public until Maria and Jaden come back from the mall with your new wardrobe. Excuse me? Yes, you *do* care. I am your fame advisor, and I will not have you prancing around like some shmuck in those rags. No, you can't just quit. You signed a contract when you entered the Lottery. Like it or not, you are this country's newest celebrity.

Oh, will you shut up already? Listen here. You know why I love this job? You know what keeps me going? Because believe it or not, I don't want to parade you from coast to coast like some prize pumpkin. I don't want to stay up all night planning your day-to-day schedule. I don't want to be here in this nasty apartment, where we can't even run a decent Internet connection. I'm only here because you—USEC's carefully-selected winner, chosen *completely* at random—are about to make millions or billions of dollars. And you signed a contract that'll pay me twenty percent of your lifelong earnings henceforth. So I suggest you suck it up, listen up, and do as I do: Smile, obey, and get rich.

(Hey! Whose phone do I hear? How many times do I have to tell you people! Ringers stay off while we're on the clock! Norm, is that your phone? Good. That would be your third strike. Kelly, phone? Show me that it's not ringing. Fine, you get to keep your job today. Where's the damn phone? Shut it off! Oh, hold on. I think it's mine.)

Fuck. It's the Secretary of Entertainment again. I gotta take this. You stay right here. Try to leave again, and I'll have to fire somebody. We don't want that, do we?

(Madame Secretary? Yes, sorry for the delay. No, I haven't seen what's trending. What do you mean? Already? We've only been online for fifteen minutes. Well, Reggie should have talked to me first. Are we sure it's a cancel call? No one's ever been canceled that quickly. What's the accusation? Yeah, I remember last year. Oh, come on! The ugly comedian?

Everyone tweeted something nasty when we canceled that guy. I don't care if he was acquitted; I know what he did to that kid. Whatever. So they're canceling my client for participating in cancel culture? Well of course *they* don't think it's hypocritical. Fine. If you're pulling the plug, I'm right there with you. Alright. Talk soon.)

Jackasses. You didn't hear any of that, did you?

(Listen up! Everyone, I need your attention! Our client has been publicly canceled. I know this is a shock, but everything is going to be fine. I have orders from the Secretary to pull the plug on this operation. Stevie, break down the servers and pack up the generator. Nancy, Andrea, don't bother cleaning up that hair on the floor. Davis, update our client's Wikipedia page with information on the controversy at hand. Benny, put our client's old clothes back where you found them. Seriously? You burned them already? Probably for the better. Ah! Maria and Jaden, right on time. Head back to the mall, return all those clothes. I hope you have the receipts. Francine, where's my water bottle? Owen! Cancel the wig order. Robin, Tom, Jamie, you know what to do. We're writing hit pieces now, so gather as much dirt as you can. Reggie, delete our client's Twitter account. Henry, I'm sorry about your ad campaign, but you've got a bigger storm coming with those sketchy energy drinks. Tamara, you hear me too? Stop drinking that garbage. Gertrude, cancel the morning show appearances. Oh, *G.M.A.* already pulled the climate activist? Whatever, they'll find someone better. Rob, cancel the reservation at the Ritz. Cynthia, I want two more pills crushed into my water, immediately. And Gene, you're fired.)

As for you, well, I think you got what you wanted. Since you didn't opt-in to a cancelation insurance policy, your contract with USEC is now void. You're no longer entitled to any monetary compensation, and we might sue you for lost time and financial damages. Oh, don't be such a baby about it! People get canceled every day. Look on the bright side! You're not famous anymore. Keep walking around wearing whatever clothes you drag up from the far corner of your bedroom—except for the ones we burned, I mean. Keep styling your hair as you like it—once it all grows back, of course. And keep *talking* to whomever you like— just not your crush from earlier today, since Reggie already sent that breakup text for you.

Well, I should be going. USEC will have to pick a secondary winner for this month, which means they'll send us on a new assignment any second. Have a great day. Sorry for the mess.

(Who else is ready to go home? Oh, I know. What a loser.)

STANDOFF

The midday peace on Cedar Drive breaks with a gust of November air. Stained glass lawn ornaments twirl. Tiny garden fountains gurgle. Inside a home on the north side of the block, a turkey roasts in an oven. A line of parked SUVs adorns the curb at the edge of the fine-trimmed lawn. Inside the house, eager relatives wander from living room to dining room, kitchen to foyer and back again while they munch on Triscuits and pre-cut carrot sticks.

A beer-bellied man in a blue Polo grows tired of walking loops with his chatty aunts, uncles, nieces, and nephews. He nods to his wife, who stands idly in their kitchen. His mother hobbles back and forth from the table to the kitchen drawers, hoarding silverware and spreading it across a fashionable autumn tablecloth. Retelling the account of her stint as a cooking student in Connecticut, she pushes past her new daughter-in-law, who smiles weakly. Preferring to let them fight it out, the Polo man plops himself down in front of the football game in the living room.

In the basement, on a couch directly below, the man's son mashes buttons on an Xbox remote. There's not much else for him to do. He can't even take Call of Duty off mute, thanks to his little sister and their young cousins running around. He finds the basement—his newfound retreat—much less secluded today. Besides, his *real* home is eighty miles southeast where his mother lives. The woman fighting his grandma in the kitchen upstairs is his new stepmother, and he hasn't figured out how to talk to her yet. He'd rather just go home. Or play Xbox. But for the first time, it's Dad's year for Thanksgiving, and there's nothing he can do about that.

The doorbell rings. The Polo man's father, a heavy-breathing war veteran, huffs towards the front door expecting his youngest daughter with a platter of deviled eggs. Instead, he opens the door to two men carrying assault rifles—newer than the ones he saw in Vietnam, but not so different altogether. But this is south-central Pennsylvania, not Saigon.

The veteran nods to the men, whose bulletproof vests say *S.W.A.T.* They mean no harm, they say, they only want to use his bathroom. The veteran hollers for his new daughter-in-law, who jogs from the battleground kitchen into the foyer. She too expects her new sister-in-law with the platter of deviled eggs, and this surprise is unwelcome. Even on Thanksgiving, she'd never let a stranger use their bathroom. Strangers don't come to the neighborhood, anyway. She and the Polo man didn't spend the better part of a million dollars for a house that gets *strangers* on its doorstep. However, upon seeing the machine guns, she decides to amend the stranger policy.

The officers' boots clop across the dark hardwood, parting the sea of extended family and mixing the smells of rubber and iron with cinnamon and ham. The veteran's wife jumps backward, holding up two handfuls of spoons innocently. Two uncles point fingers away from themselves in the direction of the powder room. One little cousin asks an officer if they're in trouble. Not at all, the man assures her, promising to explain everything in a moment.

A few minutes later, the Polo man descends the basement steps and rounds up the rest of the kids. His son reluctantly pauses Call of Duty and sulks away from the couch. The Polo man tells them all to stay inside and stay away from the windows. One of the little cousins asks why. He relays the message of the officers: There's a man with a gun nearby. His niece and nephew gasp. His daughter runs straight to the nearest window, and his son asks to go out and see. The Polo man raises his voice because the situation is serious, and they should be thankful for the safety of the house they're in.

Upstairs, the football game remains unwatched. The veteran's wife finishes setting the table and joins her husband at the edge of the foyer to watch the street. On an ordinary November afternoon, Cedar Drive might see a few leaf piles, parked Jeeps, or roving bicycles. Today, a massive caravan blocks the street from end-to-end. The guests' cars on each curb are double-parked by a sudden armada: A police cruiser at the front, then an armored S.W.A.T. van with jumbo wheels, a shiny black panel truck marked *Negotiation Unit*, an idle ambulance, another S.W.A.T. van (this one a deep green), two more police cruisers, one more panel truck labeled *Tactical Unit*, and a line of three police cars at the edge of the block. Behind their line of flashing lights, two white news vans raise their satellite dishes on antenna poles that tower over the houses. *Channel 44* and *Channel 20*, they say. The grandparents monitor the situation while munching on plates of miniature pretzels.

It's a hostage situation, one officer explains while his partner takes a piss. In one house at the opposite end of the Cedar Drive, a deranged man is holding his wife and children at gunpoint. Everything is going to be perfectly alright. The officers and tactical teams have parked on this side of the block, just beyond his view, so they won't provoke him. It's a very fluid situation, apparently, and everyone pretends to understand whatever that means. Once finished relieving themselves, the officers take their guns and return to the swarm of activity outside.

The Polo man's wife slides the supermarket turkey from the oven and displays it on a granite countertop. Her relatives rush to tell her how lovely it looks and smells, then how sure they are that it'll taste as wonderful. The landline rings, and the Polo man pushes his beer belly past everyone to pick up the call. He gasps. There will be no deviled eggs this year, he announces. His sister is trapped outside the police perimeter, and the officers won't let anyone in or out of the Cedar Drive block. He asks her to try negotiating with the tactical negotiators. He suggests that she tell them she has a platter of eggs, and to give the S.W.A.T. men samples if that's what it takes. She hangs up the phone and tries this, but the officer says he's a vegan.

After hearing about the hostages, the boy in the basement shuts off the Xbox. Watching the hostage situation sounds much more fun. He brandishes a Nerf gun and guards the basement's backdoor. Checking twice to make sure that everyone's gone upstairs, he pulls the door open and dashes out into the back yard. He carefully ducks beyond the view of the officers on the street, then shuffles behind a neighbor's fence. Through the porch window of the house next door, he sees another happy family settling down at an ornamented kitchen table for their holiday meal. Hopping a fence into the next yard, the story is the same.

The boy's father, much less afraid, struts defiantly onto his front lawn and demands to speak with one of the officers. They tell him to go back inside. He tells them it's okay, he watches police procedurals and knows how these things are done. One of the officers from the county sheriff's department steps off the street and politely guides him back towards the house. From the open foyer, seven aunts and uncles sip their wine glasses nervously. The Polo man tells the officer that his sister is stuck outside the perimeter and needs to bring in the deviled eggs. Fine, the officer relents. He radios for someone to escort the egg-plate woman down the street. The Polo man asks his wife to take a photo of him from the foyer, with all the police vehicles in the background. He'll post it on Facebook later. He always wanted to be a cop.

Down the street, a police negotiator stands outside a house with a megaphone. He tells the man inside that they're not going to hurt anyone, as long as he puts down his weapon. A sniper on a neighbor's porch aims his crosshairs through a window, seeking the man inside. The boy with his Nerf gun follows the blaring sound of the megaphone and gazes across the street at the gunman's house. It looks just like all the others, including his own. He crosses the deck of a winterized pool, then another backyard before sneaking across the street. He can't believe how much it feels like Call of Duty. The boy follows the steep hill of a drainage pit until he reaches the back of the gunman's house. Clutching his plastic weapon in both hands, he peeks through a window at the horror inside.

After taking one photo and shooing her husband back indoors, the boy's stepmother hauls the turkey to the dining room table. Having run out of Triscuits a while ago, the crowd of hungry adults files into the room and seizes their chairs. In the kitchen's overflow seating, the kids eat off paper plates. The boy's little sister joins the rowdy kitchen crew. She thinks it's no use talking with any of the cousins—they're so young, what do they know?—but talking with the adults couldn't be any better—the adults won't talk about Disney princesses, Taylor Swift, or even glitter makeup. So she sits with the other kids but doesn't talk at all; she just piles stuffing onto a paper plate. At long last, her aunt stumbles through the front door with her deviled eggs. No one's there to greet her.

The girl samples a slice of turkey and spits it into a fabric napkin. Her dad circles through the kitchen to check on all the kids and break away from his new in-laws. He tells his daughter to eat the turkey. I don't like turkey, she whines. But it looks perfectly good to eat, doesn't it? Say thank you. Where's your brother? Go get him from downstairs.

At the dining room table, the veteran's eyes dart to the window. Everyone else hears it next: A series of popping gunshots echo up the street. The engine of one S.W.A.T. van roars to life. They all consider running to the windows, and they all would, but no one dares break the lovely image of a family Thanksgiving. The turkey is wonderful, says the Polo man after forcing another dry bite down his throat. His new wife smiles. They look adorable—perfectly polished like the new silverware. The veteran misses the old silverware. In a house at the end of the street, the man pressing a handgun to his wife's temple misses the way things used to be.

The sniper, sights on him, misses nothing.

The girl with her plate of stuffing searches the whole basement—even the closet where she knows she might find her Christmas presents—but he's gone. Her brother is nowhere in the house. She remembers how badly he wanted to go look outside. She heard the gunshots, just like everyone else. Despite her age, she knows what those sound like. She hurries up the stairs to raise the alarm, but the back door of the basement bursts open.

Her brother—shaken but unharmed—runs inside, tosses his Nerf gun to the floor, and slumps against the wall. A moment later, he begins to cry. She asks him what happened. What did you see out there?

I'll be upstairs in a few minutes, he tells her. Leave me alone.

The next day, a real estate agent on Cedar Drive bribes local news channels *44* and *20* not air any information about the standoff. A banker next-door to the gunman blackmails the local paper to delete any story they planned for the Sunday edition (he knows that the editor-in-chief is having an affair with the sports editor). The Polo man decides not to post his photo on Facebook. He prints it on glossy paper and tucks it away in the drawer of his nightstand.

His son bikes to the end of the block after the police brigade clears overnight. The gunman's house still looks just like all the others: Neatly trimmed lawn, brick double-garage, hanging metal ornaments on the porch, mulch beds of manicured flowers, and a blue security sign near the mailbox. Someone's *already* fixed the window that he watched the sniper shatter. There's no blood or bullet holes to show for it. Someone's even taken in the mail from the box. The boy searches for a chunk of asphalt to lob at a window—just to make it look like something, anything, happened here—but the street is newly finished with sour-smelling black pavement.

Back at his house, the boy asks his father what happened to the man with the gun. He got the help he needs, the Polo man lies. And his family is moving to Florida, so we'll get new neighbors in that empty house.

So is everything okay now?

Yes, everything is perfect.

And I can go home to Mom's? Now that the police are gone?

Good news, actually. She said you and your sister can stay the weekend.

Oh.

Is that okay?

Mmhm. And you're sure that everything else is okay, too?

The Polo man watches stillness return to Cedar Drive. Lawn ornaments stop spinning. Garden fountains gurgle softly. The boy listens patiently for his father to lie again.

Yes, he says. Everything looks absolutely perfect.

FADE TO BLACK

The Depression—which was first called The Recession—is now something worse. I don't know what we're supposed to call it. I ran out of toothpaste last month, and I know how disgusting that sounds. Believe me, it's worse than you think. I can't buy toothpaste because I have to buy food, and sometimes I can't buy food because I have to pay rent. What I really need is a new roommate. What I really need is a new job. What I *really* need is more toothpaste, but no one can have it all.

"You're still here," I remind myself in the mirror. "You're still here."

I swipe a comb through my hair, but it sticks in a wave of knots. Forget the comb. Forget the hair. I put on a hat. How about a different hat? I look like a fucking loser. Is that good? Do I want to look good? Hell, I don't even know if I want to go on this date. My aunt says that these days it's basically suicide to put yourself out there. Then again, what does she know? She hasn't left her house in six years.

"Going on a date?" My Uber driver cranes his neck to meet my eyes in the rearview.

"Yeah."

"She ugly?"

"What?" I must have misheard.

"I said, is she ugly? Cause you know, it's safer that way. You go on a date with a beautiful woman, and then—"

"Yeah, I know, but this one's a blind date. There's a new app I'm trying out."

"Brave man."

With a salute in the rearview, he drops me off at an Irish pub on sixth street. I take a look up and down the sidewalk. As I suspected, this place has become *the* Irish pub on sixth street. They've boarded up the other one; what a damn shame. A buzzing yellow streetlamp shines on its plywood armor, and on a spray-painted message: *Love is dead.* People write that fake-deep shit everywhere, like we don't already know.

"Coming inside?" Someone asks. I turn, and she's holding the pub door open for me.

"A blind date, yeah." I step inside and remove my hat on instinct. Remembering my hair, I put it back on. "Strawberry banana?"

"Excuse me?"

I blush. "Sorry, it's this stupid dating app. I'm supposed to identify my blind date with a passphrase. So I have to keep saying 'strawberry banana' until—"

"Hey!" a man calls from a table by the window. "You said strawberry banana?"

He's one of half a dozen people in the whole pub. He's clean-shaven with buzzed black hair and a dark blue hoodie. He takes a sip from a tall glass of water on the table. I smile and shake his hand, already afraid to move too quickly. We introduce ourselves, and I take the seat across from him.

"You expected a girl?" He nods towards the woman who held the door.

I shake my head. "No! I mean, a blind date from this app could be anyone for me. I'm pansexual."

He smirks. "Well no shit. You know, eighty percent of the population came out of the closet in the last five years. Beggars can't be choosers."

"It's not like that! I've been out since junior high."

"Oh, a hipster. You did it before it was cool."

I flash a grin, then quickly wipe it off my face and backpedal. All of my aunt's warnings echo in my head. I need to be more careful.

"Sorry. Am I smiling too much? I don't want to seem… I don't know."

"Don't worry," he assures me, "you have horrible teeth."

"Thanks. I recently ran out of toothpaste."

"Dope idea. I should try that too."

"Do you go on a lot of dates, then?" I don't fear the answer, either way.

"Eh, some." He shrugs, then makes eye contact with a server and gestures for another glass of water. "Unless you wanted beer?"

I shake my head. "No, not after that Times article. Did you read it? The one where they said alcohol is the real killer?"

"Oh yeah. Typical fear-mongering shit. Leave it to the media, putting every last vineyard and brewery out of business. But you gotta admit, it makes sense, doesn't it? I remember getting wasted in college, hooking up with strangers from clubs, and forgetting it all the next day."

The server slides a second glass of water onto the table in front of me. Her face says it all. She wants us to order beers or wine, or anything that'll pay to keep the lights on.

"Here," my date says. He digs in his hoodie pocket and hands her a folded five-dollar bill. "It's all I got."

"Thank you." She takes the cash and retreats to the bar. There's a pause. The pub is so damn quiet. I sip my water and strain to pick up our conversation.

"You say you forgot about all those drunken hookups, but you remember them now?"

"Okay, maybe I didn't forget *everything*." He's smiling. Fuck, I'm being too clever. My aunt would slap me. I need to tone it down. I need to say something terrible.

"I don't like your style. That's a lazy outfit."

His eyes drop to the sleeves of his hoodie. He laughs. "Thanks. I'm glad you noticed. I figure I've got no one left to impress. What about you?" There's a bold question. Harsh, even. He's a smart man. "Who do you know who's still around, I mean?"

I take a deep breath.

"My aunt, mostly. She's an agoraphobe. Been that way since, uh… Well, my grandparents were first. They disappeared right at the beginning. My mom and dad, they tried to play it safe. They separated until six years ago, but then they reunited and vanished anyway. And last year, my dumbass brother met an artist from Brooklyn. Only took them a few weeks before it happened. So yeah, just my aunt now."

"Yeah," he nods. "That's lucky, though. I've lost everybody. Like really, everyone. I was a foster kid. Put myself through college and shit. All I ever had were roommates, and one by one they were gone. Like another shitty pandemic, that's what it is."

"Literally," I add. "World Health Organization said so, didn't they?"

"Well yeah, but where's the pathogen? You can't have a pandemic without some virus to analyze under a microscope. There sure as shit isn't a vaccine! Can you imagine? But no, we don't even have any bodies left to autopsy. Who says pandemic; I say rapture."

"*Who* says pandemic?"

"Yeah, W-H-O. World Health Org—"

"Oh! Right. Funny." I take another sip of water so that I'll stop fucking smiling. "Rapture, then. So you're religious?"

"Aren't we all?" He pauses. If it's a joke, I'm still waiting for the punchline. "Like, think about it. It's been almost a decade since this thing started. At the beginning, you remember how everyone was in denial? They said, 'This can't be happening! Show me the proof!' And then the YouTube videos go up. People see this shit with their own eyes. I remember this viral video where a couple takes an elevator up the Eiffel Tower and never comes down. Okay, there's you're proof. So then what? People have no choice but to believe their eyes."

I shake my head. "But it doesn't prove that God exists."

"No, not God," he laughs. "It proves that *love* exists."

"Oh." I take another swig of water.

"Am I talking too much?"

I try to shrug, but it turns into a nod.

"Good."

"You were saying?"

He taps his foot and picks up his train of thought. "Right! So before all this, hypothetically, how did you know you were in love? How did anyone know?"

"Gut feeling, I guess. I never knew for sure."

"Exactly. No one ever figured a chemical recipe for love. No one could ever say for sure that it was a real thing, like an on-off switch. But now? Now that we have this rapture—or pandemic, whatever spooky bullshit this is—we can see it with our own eyes. We can see the *exact* moment when love exists. The instant you fall in love, well…"

He raises his glass. I clink mine against his.

"Fall in love, and you fucking disappear." When I say it, it sounds insane. That's why no one ever talks about it. We just watch the streets empty out. We watch the bars close, one by one. We watch everyone lose their jobs, run out of toothpaste, and lock themselves away. After watching the world collapse for long enough, it all becomes unspeakable. Love becomes a four-letter word.

He grimaces and finishes his water glass. "Yup. Cheers to fucking disappearing."

I straighten in my chair. "Is that your plan then? Fall in love and disappear?"

"No."

"Good. Me neither."

"Good. Why are you here, then? For meaningless sex, or is it a death wish?"

I clutch my glass and stare out the window. *You're still here*, I remind myself. But his question falls like a rock in my stomach. What was my brother thinking when he met that artist in Brooklyn? Did he want to kill himself?

"I don't know. I like talking to you. That's better than meaningless sex."

He exhales sharply. "Deathwish it is. You've got nothing left to lose."

"Oh, I've got nothing left? Speak for yourself, foster kid."

He glares at me. I glare right back. Fuck, that's eye contact. Why am I letting eye contact happen? His eyes are deep brown, almost black in the pub's light. I hate this guy. I hate his ugly blue hoodie, too. I want to hate him and be safe, end the date, go home, and never see him again. I want to wake up tomorrow, look in the mirror, and tell myself that I'm still here.

But eye contact feels so fucking good.

Before I know it, we're laughing. We're cracking up. How long can you really look at another person's eyes before you smile? Can anyone in a staring contest keep a straight face forever?

As soon as he stops laughing, he stands and pushes his chair under the table.

"Man, I gotta leave."

I rise and stow my chair too. "You know what? Me too."

"Copycat."

We leave our empty glasses at the table. I'm closer to the door, so I hold it for him. "After you."

"No, go ahead. After you."

"Knock that shit off, will you?" I'm starting to sound like him. What's that about?

"Knock what off?" He steps outside and pulls his hood over his head.

"Flirting! My aunt would say you're gonna get us both killed."

"Well you're still here, aren't you?"

I check my reflection in the pub's glass window. Still here. "Guess this means I'm not in love with you. Are you offended?"

"Man, I'm crushed." He turns and starts up the sidewalk, but I can hear the smile in his voice. Best of all, he's walking the same way as me.

Wait. What am I thinking, 'best of all?' That's not a good thing. I need to get away from this guy. He's dangerous. Funny, clever, and all the other deadly things. I need to work on Monday. I need to pay rent. I need to buy food. Never mind toothpaste, but I have responsibilities. I have a life to lead. For some reason, I do have a life, don't I?

"Oh, you're stalking me now?" He walks backwards while I catch up.

"No! I just live this way too."

"Wow, we have so much in common. Let's get married."

I punch his shoulder. "I hate you."

"Thank God. I hate you too."

I laugh again, and I don't bother hiding it. The sound echoes up the street. I haven't heard myself laugh so loud in years. Hell, I can't remember the last time I heard anyone's laugh echoing. It's a foreign, beautiful noise. It reminds me of a film I saw, ages ago. Words like rain pour from my mouth.

"Do you remember the old romance movies? The ones where the main characters hate each other for most of the film, find some magical connection, then live happily ever after? The ones where the story ends as soon as they fall in love? I remember watching one of those movies and thinking it felt so fucking poetic. There's this old idea that once you've achieved love, it's okay to just roll the credits and fade to black. People loved those movies. What ever happened to them?"

He shrugs. "People got scared. Romance became horror. Literally."

"Yeah," I sigh. "I'm fucking sick of being scared."

"Maybe that's what it is, then."

"What *what* is?"

He rolls his eyes. "Love! What if love is what happens when you stop being scared?"

He sounds like one of those fake-deep people who spray-paints their ideas across foreclosed pubs. I glare at him again.

"Are you scared?" he asks, glaring back. Eye contact. If this is the end of the movie, I don't care if we live happily ever after. If all I have is one strange moment on this sidewalk—with this man and his lazy outfit—that's okay with me.

"No," I confess. "I'm not afraid anymore."

I break our eye contact. A curtain of darkness falls over the streetlights. The empty sidewalk curls inward on itself, cradling our bodies and closing the aperture of reddish city twilight. The pub, the abandoned skyscrapers, and the whole loveless world drifts into oblivion. We disappear from that place, and without taking a single step, we arrive somewhere new.

"So there it is," he whispers. "The 'fade to black,' like one of those shitty movies."

"No," I tell him and reach for his hand in the dark. "We're still here."

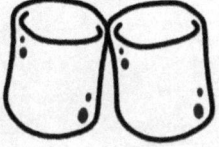

ABOUT THE AUTHOR

S.C. Giedzinski is a Brooklyn-based engineer who designs solar farms throughout the United States. Giedzinski is also an audiobook narrator and designer of open-source 3D-printing projects. Giedzinski graduated from the University of Maryland in 2021 with a B.S. in mechanical engineering and a creative writing minor.

Giedzinski's short stories have been published by the Baltimore Science Fiction Society and *Stylus* Literary Journal. Giedzinski's debut novel, *Island Rain*, is available in paperback.

www.ingramcontent.com/pod-product-compliance
Lightning Source LLC
Chambersburg PA
CBHW050154110726
47898CB00008B/2793